Holiday Magic Boomer Style

How to reset after decades of tradition

A L Manley

Ink-Twenty.Studio

Richmond, VA

Holiday Magic Boomer Style
How to Reset After Decades of Tradition
© 2025 by A L Manley

ISBN 9798993554433

Published by Ink-Twenty.Studio
Richmond, Virginia

For more information, visit Ink-Twenty.Studio

Holiday Magic Boomer Style

How to Reset After Decades of
Tradition

With the grandkids grown and living their own lives, what now?

Holidays since childhood have been a cavalcade of tradition — grandparents setting the tone, parents following suit, children learning by example, and children's children carrying bits of it forward. The garland, the glow, the chaos — every generation adding something new, keeping something old.

The lights have changed right along with the times. Those big, pointy bulbs that could practically cook a marshmallow gave way to soft, twinkling fairy lights. And the trees? In the late '50s and '60s, almost every household brought home the real thing — fresh pine scent, sticky sap, and needles in the rug until Easter. Then came the aluminum trees, shining under a rotating color wheel until A Charlie Brown Christmas made everyone feel guilty. Today, about 83% of tree-displaying households choose artificial — pre-lit, boxed, bagged, and ready to fluff next year.

Thanksgiving once marked the official start of the retail parade. Department stores were decked out like Broadway sets, and Santa didn't make his grand entrance until the Friday after. Store elves, long lines, Polaroid photos, crying babies — the works. Now the Amazon driver might toss a package on the porch wearing a Santa hat and call it festive.

Boomer, you've lived a rich slice of American history. You've watched uncles and brothers drafted into wars that outlasted their reasons. You've stood through assassinations, inaugurations, riots, marches, and speeches that shook a nation awake. The term "DEI" may sound modern, but the original faces of Affirmative Action were the real pioneers — stepping into neighborhoods, offices, and schools where their very presence rewrote the rules.

You've seen peace accords inked between Egypt and Israel at Camp David. You've watched automobiles evolve from solid steel tanks with chrome bumpers to light, plastic hybrids rolling silently on battery power.

And now, after decades of doing holidays for everyone else, it's time to do them for you.

This is the permission slip to reset — to make December fit your life, not the other way around. Keep the traditions that still sparkle, drop the ones that drain you, and add something that makes you smile. The goal isn't perfection; it's peace. Real, quiet, coffee-in-your-favorite-cup peace.

Back In The Day Part I

Before Amazon and next-day delivery, we shopped the old-fashioned way — by circling parking lots like vultures waiting for someone to back out. The holiday season kicked off the moment Thanksgiving leftovers were packed away, and by 6 A.M. on Friday morning, the streets around the malls looked like rush hour in December snow.

And we loved it.

You didn't just shop; you hunted. You dressed for battle — sneakers, coffee thermos, maybe a light jacket because it was always freezing when you went in and too hot when you came out. You grabbed a cart with a wobbly wheel and hit the aisles like a general with a mission. Back then, doorbusters meant something. They didn't just unlock the doors early — they flung them open like floodgates.

Sears and Kmart were the King and Queen of retail. Sears was the respectable one — your parents trusted Sears. Appliances, tools, holiday décor, that thick catalog with glossy pages that could double as a doorstop. And Kmart? That was the working-class hero of holiday shopping — the Blue Light Special flashing like a Vegas jackpot. You could walk in for wrapping paper and walk out with a new blender, a set of towels, and half your gift list done.

By the late seventies, malls were America's weekend playgrounds. You could meet a friend, grab a slice of pizza, and walk under skylights so shiny you'd swear they piped in sunshine. And when the Christmas season rolled around, they went full Broadway — garland on every railing, music on loop, fake snow that somehow still got in your hair.

Then came Walmart — the friendly neighbor who showed up in 1962, quietly built an empire through the seventies, and by the early nineties had taken over Main Street entirely. Before long, Sears was fading, Kmart was faltering, and Walmart was swallowing them whole one rollback at a time. Sam's Club opened in 1983 — the "buy it in bulk" cousin who made you feel grown-up for owning a membership card. And Costco followed close behind, offering samples so good you could eat lunch without ever checking out.

But back in the 70s and 80s, you didn't need a barcode scanner to feel the magic. You needed a cup of hot chocolate, a car full of bags, and a house that smelled like pine and Scotch tape.

It was a different kind of joy — earned through the hustle, not the click.

Back In The Day Part II — The 90s Shift

By the 1990s, everything was speeding up — cars, computers, cable TV, and kids who suddenly had opinions about everything. The world was on the move, and for Boomers raising families, it felt like one long sprint between the school carpool and Blockbuster's return bin.

You still did your shopping in person, but now you had choices — Walmart was open 24 hours, malls stayed busy seven days a week, and those new "supercenters" popped up like mushrooms after rain. Sam's Club and Costco were membership must-haves, a sign that you were running a household, not a lemonade stand. You bought bulk because it made sense

— paper towels stacked to the ceiling, a ten-pound bag of sugar you'd never finish, and enough batteries to power a small city.

You might've been driving a Ford Taurus, a Chevy Caprice, or if you were feeling sporty, a Pontiac Grand Am — the kind of car that looked fast even when it wasn't. Gas was about a dollar a gallon, and a road trip didn't require a loan or a podcast playlist. You had a glove box full of maps, a cup of gas-station coffee, and maybe a cassette of Fleetwood Mac or Tina Turner.

At home, the TV was the heartbeat of the house. The Nielsen Ratings decided what America watched, and that mattered. Thursday nights were sacred — NBC's "Must-See TV." Cheers, The Cosby Show, Friends, Seinfeld, Frasier — you knew the lineup by heart. Friday nights were for Dallas and Falcon Crest, and if you were up past midnight, Saturday Night Live gave you your dose of irreverence before church the next morning.

Commercials were an art form. They didn't interrupt your show — they were the show. The Budweiser frogs, the dancing California Raisins, the Energizer Bunny that kept going and going, and Coca-Cola convincing us all to "Open Happiness." And that's exactly what we did — usually in a can, poured over crushed ice in a tall glass.

Movies were communal — real events. You didn't stream; you showed up. You stood in line for Titanic, Forrest Gump, Pretty Woman, or The Bodyguard. You bought a ticket, grabbed buttery popcorn, and found your seat in the dark, where for two hours, life paused. Remember when Jurassic Park roared onto the screen? People gasped. Nobody checked their phone — because you didn't have one.

And the fashion? Oh, the 90s had personality. Shoulder pads were easing their way out, denim was king, and The Gap was the mothership. Your closet probably held at least one turtleneck, a chambray shirt, or a pair of acid-wash jeans you still swear looked good. Reebok high-tops, scrunchies, flannel, leather jackets — we didn't just wear clothes; we made statements.

Sports were just as iconic. Joe Montana and the 49ers owned the Super Bowl spotlight. Baseball had Mr. October — Reggie Jackson — when October meant October. The World Series wasn't interrupted by snowstorms or November calendars; it ended before Halloween candy went stale. Michael Jordan ruled the NBA, and Boomer parents ruled the remote.

The soundtrack of the 90s could make a grown man nostalgic — Whitney, Madonna, Prince, Springsteen, George Michael, Phil Collins, and the smooth voice of Luther Vandross on Sunday mornings. You danced in the kitchen, vacuumed to Gloria Estefan, and cried to Bette Midler.

Life was full. Tangible. You knew your neighbors. You knew your mailman. You knew how to fix a VCR that ate your tape — you just blew on it and prayed. The internet wasn't running your life yet; it was something your kid explained to you once and you said, "That's nice, honey."

Back in the day, you didn't need Wi-Fi to feel connected. You had a kitchen phone with a cord long enough to reach the laundry room, a paper calendar on the fridge, and a mailbox stuffed with holiday cards. When company came over, you brewed a pot of coffee — real coffee, none of that foam nonsense — and sat at the table till someone said, "Well, I better head home before it gets dark."

Now that was the good ol' days.

Pop Culture Part III—Candy Wrapper Memories

Long before streaming, hashtags, and Bluetooth speakers, the Boomers lived in stereo — vinyl, transistor radios, and jukeboxes that swallowed quarters like candy. Music wasn't background noise; it was a pulse.

Elvis Presley hit the scene in 1956, hips first, and America collectively gasped. Mothers clutched pearls, fathers muttered about "that boy," and teenagers went full swoon. Rock 'n' roll had officially arrived — scandalous, electric, and alive. The Ed Sullivan Show didn't just make Elvis famous; it rewired the American sound.

By the early '60s, Motown was the soul of the nation. The Temptations, The Supremes, Marvin Gaye, Smokey Robinson — that Detroit rhythm made you move whether you meant to or not. Even the shyest wallflower could sway to My Girl or Ain't No Mountain High Enough. It wasn't just music; it was unity. For the first time, radio brought Black and white listeners together, singing the same lyrics, tapping the same beat, shoulder to shoulder at the sock hop.

Then came The Beatles. Four boys from Liverpool who made us want moptops and mod dresses, even if we couldn't spell "Beatlemania." They showed up on Ed Sullivan in 1964, and suddenly every garage in America had a kid with a guitar and a dream. The Rolling Stones, Jimi Hendrix, Janis Joplin —

the sound grew bolder, the hair grew longer, and the youth movement turned into a force.

The late '60s and early '70s brought protest songs and power chords. Vietnam wasn't just a war; it was a generational scar — drafted brothers, missing neighbors, families holding their breath through nightly news updates. But out of that pain came anthems — Blowin' in the Wind, Fortunate Son, Give Peace a Chance. Music carried the grief, the anger, and the hope that someday we'd all come home.

By the mid-'70s, disco balls replaced protest signs. Studio 54 shimmered, polyester ruled, and everybody owned at least one pair of bell-bottoms that could double as sails. If you didn't know the Hustle, you learned it — usually in a living room cleared of furniture. The Bee Gees, Donna Summer, and Earth, Wind & Fire taught us that a beat could heal just as well as a ballad.

Then came the '80s — MTV's neon decade. Suddenly, music wasn't just heard; it was seen. Michael Jackson moonwalked, Madonna made lace gloves cool, and Prince turned purple into a religion. We still slow danced to Lionel Richie and powered through workouts with Olivia Newton-John. Boomboxes on shoulders, Walkmans on hips — if you had batteries, you had freedom.

Movies and TV shaped us just as much. From The Graduate to Rocky, from All in the Family to The Golden Girls, we saw ourselves grow up in real time. Nielsen ratings actually meant something back then — a single night's numbers could crown a hit or bury a series. The Super Bowl wasn't just a game; it was an event, with commercials that people quoted at work the next day.

Pop culture gave Boomers an identity — not polished, not perfect, but authentic. You learned empathy through Motown, rebellion through rock, resilience through the war years, and joy through disco and MTV. Every song, every show, every headline became a mile marker in a life well-lived.

So when the early 2000s rolled around — with streaming, smartphones, and "content" instead of art — Boomers could smile knowingly. Because you'd already danced through every revolution that mattered.

As the 20th century wound down, the soundtrack shifted again. The hair got shorter, the jeans higher-waisted, and the music moved from vinyl to CD to something called "digital." Boomers, now juggling teenagers, mortgages, and PTA meetings, watched their own history become nostalgia — classic rock stations, "best of the '70s" albums, and reunion tours that sold out faster than they could say "Where's my lighter?"

And while the beat of the times changed, so did the pace of life. Technology began sneaking into the living room, and suddenly the future was knocking — cordless phones, home computers, that strange new thing called "email." The millennium was coming, and the Boomers were standing right in the middle of it — wiser, worldlier, still dancing, but now keeping one eye on retirement funds and one on the headlines.

The world they built was speeding toward something new, and they were about to witness it all.

Back In The Day Part IV— Crossing the Millennium

By the early 2000s, Boomers had raised their families, paid off mortgages, and learned how to program the VCR… just in time for the DVD player to take over. Life moved fast — faster than a dial-up modem on a good day — and suddenly the world you'd known for fifty years was morphing into something you could barely recognize.

Your kids were in college or just starting families of their own. They shopped online, texted instead of called, and didn't need a mall map to find a deal. You watched as Black Friday became Cyber Monday, and the parking-lot parade turned into UPS trucks humming through neighborhoods.

Amazon wasn't a bookstore anymore — it was the everything store. Walmart had a website. Sears had… regrets. Kmart was fading like an old Polaroid, and malls that once felt like city centers started to echo with empty storefronts and distant holiday music.

Television had changed, too. Remember when you had three remotes and still couldn't find the right one? Now you were streaming — or at least trying to. TiVo was a miracle until Netflix stole its thunder. The Nielsen Ratings stopped ruling the roost because everyone was watching something different, at a different time, in a different way.

Cars looked sleeker, quieter — and suddenly there was talk of electric vehicles, even though most of us still trusted a good V-8 under the hood. Minivans gave way to SUVs, and cup holders multiplied like rabbits.

And the holidays? Well, they started to feel a little different. Your children were grown, your house wasn't quite as loud, and "family gatherings" sometimes meant Zoom calls and shipped presents instead of the chaos of wrapping paper on the floor.

That's when Boomers began to realize something important — tradition had changed shape. It wasn't gone, just… lighter. Faster. Less about the spectacle, more about the connection. The world had gone digital, but you hadn't lost your sense of magic — you'd simply learned to adapt it.

You still put up a tree — maybe smaller, maybe pre-lit — and hung the ornaments that had survived since the Reagan years. You still played the same holiday albums, even if the music now came from a Bluetooth speaker instead of a stereo system with a stack of CDs.

The beauty of being a Boomer is this: you've lived through every evolution — and somehow, you still make December feel like December. You may not line up at dawn for door busters anymore, but you know how to make the season matter. You've earned your place in the timeline — part nostalgia, part wisdom, all heart.

Part V – Boomers: The Real Glow-Up

Somewhere between disco balls and digital downloads, the Boomers grew up — and grew into themselves. The same generation that once snuck out with a six-pack and a transistor radio now goes to bed with magnesium, eye cream, and a white-noise app.

The 10-year class reunion was a fashion show — everyone still had their original knees, and the biggest brag was who drove the newest car. At the 20-year mark, you started noticing names missing from the address list — and at the 30th, you quietly admitted that you didn't recognize half the people because everyone had changed hair colors. The 40th reunion brought reading glasses, and the 50th? That one felt like a miracle. You looked around and thought, "Damn, we made it."

Part VI – Resetting the Season

So here we are — a generation that's danced under disco balls, marched for peace, raised families, and learned to FaceTime the grandkids. The tree might be smaller now, the lights easier to hang, and the music coming from a playlist instead of a turntable — but the heart of it all hasn't changed.

What has changed is you.
And that means it's time to celebrate the holidays your way — lighter, freer, with less fuss and more joy.

By then, life had softened around the edges. The kids were gone, the house echoed a little, and you started hearing the term empty nester whispered like a diagnosis. But the truth? It wasn't empty — it was peaceful. You could finally eat dinner at eight, travel on a whim, and take your time in the grocery store without somebody tugging on your sleeve.

Work slowed down, or stopped altogether. Retirement wasn't just a word on an HR brochure anymore — it was a new chapter. Some Boomers leaned into it with glee: golf, gardening, pickleball, cruises, naps. Others resisted with the energy of a protest march — part-time jobs, consulting gigs, "projects" that conveniently lasted all year.

And then came the mirror.

You woke up one day and realized your hair was lying to you — or maybe you were lying to it. The grays crept in like uninvited guests, and suddenly every salon visit came with choices: go natural, go neutral, or go platinum and pretend it's on purpose.

Stylists became therapists with foils. They listened, they comforted, and they mixed color formulas like chemists at NASA. You sat there sipping coffee, pretending to read a magazine, while silently negotiating with your reflection: "Just one more year. I'm not ready yet."

But some women — brave, beautiful, and unbothered — said, "To hell with it." They walked into the world silver-haired and stunning, radiating that particular brand of confidence that comes from surviving disco, childbirth, and dial-up internet.

Meanwhile, men were buying "natural-looking" hair color kits and pretending it was shampoo. Commercials started promising a youthful glow for women and distinguished confidence for men — which is marketing code for "we know you're aging, but we'll help you do it in HD." Beards turned silver, temples frosted, and suddenly salt-and-pepper was sexy again.

Then the real twist hit: your children became parents. The very ones who used to roll their eyes at your rules now called for advice about car seats, sleep schedules, and whether toddlers really need organic everything. You became grandparents — the wise ones, the soft-touch ones, the "I've got snacks in my purse" ones. And just like that, the cycle reset.

You were no longer the middle of the story — you were the roots. Watching your grown kids juggle life gave you perspective. You smiled, remembering how you once did the same dance — just without Wi-Fi or DoorDash.

So here you are. A Boomer. Stronger than your joints admit, wiser than your kids think, and still showing up with good hair, great stories, and better snacks. You've earned your laugh lines. You've earned your peace. You've even earned the right to skip the reunion if you damn well feel like it.

Because this chapter of life? It's not about going back — it's about owning exactly who you've become.

Part VII — The Middle Child

(The Younger Boomer)

Baby Boomers officially run from 1946 to 1964.

Twenty years that held everything from post-war sidewalks and Sunday dinners to mini-skirts, moon landings, Motown, and microwaves.

And inside that twenty-year stretch, there are two Boomer experiences.

The older Boomers — the early wave — were the ones standing on the front steps when the world changed. They remember when "good manners" were non-negotiable, when women were called "girls" even in the workplace, when church was the anchor and the family dinner table was the daily meeting room.

Then — almost overnight — everything shifted.
Clothes loosened. Rules bent. Language cracked open.
Love became political. Voices got louder. And music — Lord, the music — became a revolution you could dance to.

Older Boomers didn't hear about change — they lived it while it was happening.
They saw the before and the after, and they remember the moment the country took a deep breath and never let it out again.

Now the younger Boomers — the ones born in the late fifties and early sixties — they were the bridge.

Not quite the fire-starters.
Not quite the new generation that came after.

They arrived in the middle of evolution.
Not handed the past. Not handed the future.
Handed the transition.

And that's why they sometimes felt like the middle child at the holiday table — watching everyone else carve turkey and carve history, while they just tried to stay balanced on the shifting carpet.

The older Boomer remembers life before the change.
The younger Boomer remembers life while everything was changing.

Two Boomer hearts. Same generation.
Different weather.

And now here we are, later in life, watching our own bodies do what the world did — shift, adjust, negotiate.

The older Boomer has already walked through the fire — the night sweats, the body's "surprise redecoration," the moment the mirror said, "We're aging, darling — let's do it with style."
There is a calm in that. A knowing. A peace that settles into the bones like a favorite chair.

The younger Boomer?
Still mid-stride.
Still renegotiating with hormones, joints, sleep cycles, appetites — physical, emotional, and otherwise.
Still saying, "Well hold on now, I wasn't finished being cute."
And the universe whispering back, "Oh, sweetheart — you're still cute. Just differently."

And then — right behind them — comes Gen X, our children.

The self-starters. The lock-the-door-on-your-way-in kids.

Raised during recessions, cable TV, divorce becoming normal, microwaved dinners and "figure it out."

They don't ask for instructions; they assume there aren't any.

So in one family you can have:

One Boomer seasoned and centered.
One Boomer still adjusting and negotiating.
And a Gen Xer who says, "I love you, but please don't call me before 9 a.m. or after 9 p.m."

Different rhythms.
Same table.

Same love — just expressed in different languages.

The beauty of being a Boomer — older or younger — is this:
You've lived through waves of change, and you're still evolving.
Still learning how to love yourself in new skin.
Still learning how to be gentle with a body that remembers your youth a little better than it can reenact it.

There is no "too late."
There is only now.
And you — older, younger, somewhere in the middle — are still very much becoming.

Part VIII — The Season of Big Decisions

(Money, houses, and where your heart wants to live)

There's a quiet moment that sneaks up somewhere in the early-to-mid 60s when the calendar and the calculator sit down at the same table. You've lived a whole life; now it's time to make the numbers behave. For Boomers, the first fork in the road usually has a big neon sign: Social Security. At 62, you can claim— yes, that's still the earliest age—and plenty of folks do because the world doesn't always wait politely. But claiming early means a permanent haircut on the monthly check; for people whose full retirement age is 67, starting at 62 can trim the benefit by roughly 30%. Wait it out and the opposite happens: after you hit full retirement age, your check grows with delayed retirement credits—about 8% more for each full year you hold off, stopping at 70. The same program that cut our grandparents' checks now rewards patience like a virtue—and sometimes, like a luxury.

Of course, Social Security isn't the only dance partner. That 401(k) you fed for decades starts looking back at you like a well-stocked pantry. The rules changed recently: Required Minimum Distributions (RMDs) generally begin at 73 now, with the option to push that first one to April 1 of the following year—though doing so often forces two taxable withdrawals in the same year. And coming in 2033, the RMD starting age rises again to 75, giving late-career Boomers more runway to plan, convert, or glide into retirement at their own speed. Miss an RMD and the IRS can get salty—there's a steep penalty (it can be reduced if you fix it quickly), so this is one of those "set a reminder and breathe easy" situations.

Then there are annuities—the word people whisper like it's either a secret weapon or a trap door. Truth? They can be both. Annuities can turn a slice of savings into a predictable paycheck you can't outlive, which for many is priceless peace of mind. But they come in flavors (fixed, variable, indexed), they have fees and surrender schedules, and the bells and whistles (riders) aren't free. Fixed and indexed versions aim for steadier rides; variable throws you onto the market roller coaster with upside and downside. The headline is simple: if you want guaranteed income and will actually sleep better with it, great—just read the contract twice and the sales pitch not at all.

While the dollars introduce themselves, the house clears its throat. That big, beautiful home that held teenagers and Thanksgiving may suddenly feel like it's wearing your joints instead of you wearing it. Do you keep the guest rooms for grandkid invasions, or do you trade square footage for sunlight and less stress? "Downsizing" used to sound like surrender; now it can feel like strategy: fewer steps, lower bills, more time for the life you actually want. If your heart says "keep the gathering place," keep it. If your knees file a formal complaint, listen to them. There's no moral victory in climbing stairs you don't need.

Maybe the answer isn't smaller—it's different. America has been inventing "55-plus" living since before bell-bottoms: Youngtown, Arizona launched the first age-restricted community back in 1954; Del Webb's Sun City took the idea mainstream in 1960 with golf carts and neighbors who waved back. What started as a novelty became a model for active-adult neighborhoods coast to coast.

And then there's The Villages—Florida's grand carnival of retirement—so large it spans multiple towns and keeps showing up in the census as America's fastest-growing metro. It's part golf-cart utopia, part small city, with entertainment every night and enough clubs to keep even the most extroverted Boomer booked till Tuesday. For some, it's heaven on a pickleball paddle; for others, it's too much party and not enough porch. That's the beauty of this season—you choose your volume. Census.gov+1

Another choice whispers from the phone: move closer to the kids. For some, it's a slam dunk—holidays together, school plays, emergency

"Can you help?" texts answered in minutes. For others, proximity complicates old rhythms, and visits work better than daily drop-ins. The rule of thumb: go where your life feels bigger, not smaller. If your joy grows when you picture Sunday dinners and soccer games, there's your answer. If you see your independence shrinking, honor that too.

The truth hiding in all these decisions is simple: this isn't about shrinking your life. It's about right-sizing it. Claim at 62 if that protects your peace and pays your bills; wait if you can and want the larger check. Use an annuity if guaranteed income helps you breathe; skip it if fees make you itch. Keep the big house if it holds your stories; trade it for sunlight and a shorter to-do list if that lets you live more and maintain less.

And if anyone asks what you're doing, tell them the truth:

"I'm editing my life for the good parts."

Part IX — The Quiet Season of the Body

Menopause for women is not just hot flashes and "mood swings," no matter what the jokes say. It's sleep that shifts without permission, metabolism that slows like it's considering retirement too, and a body that decides to rearrange itself while you're sleeping. It's libido that sometimes clocks out early and sometimes comes roaring back like it's 1993 and you're in a sundress with a good bra and no curfew.

It touches identity.
It touches memory.
It touches who you thought you were and who you may still become.

It is grief and relief living in the same house. It is losing things you thought were permanent, while gaining wisdom you didn't know you were missing.

Now men—yes, there is something parallel. They don't call it menopause (and don't try that word on them unless you're prepared for spirited discussion). The clinical term is andropause. But unlike ours, which can arrive like weather, theirs is a slow shift—time tapping them lightly on the shoulder each year after forty.

Testosterone changes in a gradual slide. Not dramatic. Just steady. And they feel it in ways they rarely say out loud: energy that doesn't quite arrive on command, drive (sexual and otherwise) that needs coaxing instead of bursting, strength and muscle tone that step back unless maintained, confidence that pauses before it speaks, sleep that flickers like an old lamp dimming and brightening.

None of this means decline.
It simply means change.

And here is where relationships get tender:

One partner may have already come through the fire—centered, calmer, done wrestling the body and now committed to partnering with it. The other may still be in the middle of the renegotiation—figuring out how to live in a body that now uses a quieter language.

This is where gentleness matters.
This is where grace matters.
This is where we stop treating aging like a loss and start treating it like a season.

A woman who has come through menopause carries a kind of knowing calm.

A man moving through andropause is learning to inhabit a quieter strength—the kind that doesn't have to prove itself.

When both recognize the shift—in themselves and in each other—love doesn't fade.
It deepens.
It softens.
It becomes honest.

And if you are navigating this chapter alone, the same applies inward.

You do not have to "bounce back."
You do not have to "stay young."
You do not have to fight nature.

You simply stay alive in your own life.
Curious. Open. Kind to the bones and joints that carried you through decades.
Willing to laugh softly at yourself.

Willing to rest.
Willing to enjoy.

Your body is not betraying you.
Your body is saying, gently:

I am still here.
Be here with me.

Part X — The After-Retirement Stage

Staying Active, Even When the Body Says "Wait a Minute"

You may still feel 37 on the inside, but your knees, hips, and lower back are quietly taking notes. The good news: you don't need to outrun a teenager or bench-press your grandkid into the next century — you just need to move with intention.

The Centers for Disease Control and Prevention (CDC) says that for adults 65 +, the sweet spot is about 150 minutes of moderate aerobic activity per week, plus at least two days of muscle-strengthening, plus a little balance work. What that looks like in real life:

Brisk walks — you'll be surprised how much 30 minutes five days a week does for you.

Two strength sessions — even body-weight moves count: squats, wall push-ups, light resistance bands.

Balance drills — heel-to-toe walking, single-leg stands, maybe yoga or Tai Chi so you don't unexpectedly meet the floor.

The payoff? Better heart health, better brain health, fewer falls, and more independence. So yes: your mind says "marathon," your body says "mini-marathon," and between them you find the perfect stride.

Keeping the Mind Sharp — Because Your Story Isn't Over

You've been through wars (literal and cultural), negotiated careers and home lives, and now your brain still wants purpose. Good — give it some. Movement helps the brain, but so does curiosity.

Here are fun ways to keep your mind in the game:

Take a class you never thought you'd enjoy — pottery, photography, watercolor, even improv comedy.

Learn a new tech skill with your grandkids as coaches — they'll love the role reversal.

Volunteer your hard-earned wisdom: mentoring, library reading hours, museum docent programs, or board service.

Play mind games that don't feel like homework — bridge, mahjong, puzzles, word games, even the occasional video game if it makes you laugh.

The key: don't just use your brain — challenge it. Novelty matters.

Social Connections Matter More Than You Think

Here's the serious truth, wrapped in plain language. There's a silent danger out there: loneliness. It doesn't make headlines, but it quietly breaks hearts — literally. The CDC warns that social isolation raises the risk of heart disease, stroke, diabetes, depression, and dementia.

Translation: friends and laughter are as essential as vitamins. Connection doesn't have to mean crowds or constant parties; it just means presence. A neighbor to wave to. A club to belong to. A weekly lunch date. A phone call that lasts longer than a text thread.

It doesn't have to be The Villages. It can be a coffee group, a church circle, a walking buddy, or an art class. The goal is simple — stay visible, stay viable, stay you.

Diet, Drinks & Other Good Habits

Let's talk about the daily stuff that keeps you feeling like yourself:

Diet: Your metabolism may have turned into a polite snail. Lean proteins, colorful veggies, and plenty of water keep the engine purring.

Alcohol: Still fine, in moderation. One glass of wine can feel festive; three can feel like regret.

Smoking: If you still smoke — stop. The benefits of quitting show up almost immediately.

Sleep: Aim for seven to eight hours. You've earned it.

Check-ups: Know your numbers. Don't wait until your doctor sends a search party.

Health isn't about restriction anymore — it's about strategy.

Pets: Companionship with a Tail (or a Purr)

Let's be honest — sometimes the best medicine has fur. A pet can fill your home with warmth and purpose faster than any self-help book. Morning walk with a dog, quiet coffee while a cat curls on your lap — built-in companionship and a reason to get up, get out, and stay moving.

And here's a tip from the heart: you don't have to start with a full-blown puppy. Puppies are like toddlers with teeth — adorable, exhausting, and ready to redecorate your shoes. A rescue dog from the pound, or a calm senior pet, can be the perfect fit. They're grateful, gentle, and already know the meaning of "sit."

Or maybe it's a cat — low-maintenance, elegant, and perfectly fine with your slower mornings. Cats judge no one, nap often, and remind you that sometimes the best activity is stillness.

A pet doesn't just keep you company — it keeps you connected. You'll meet other pet owners, trade stories, share laughs, and maybe even swap treats. That's community disguised as companionship.

Still Vibrant, Still You

Here's the thing no chart or study can capture: you're still here, still curious, still laughing. The body might creak, the mirror might hesitate, but the spark hasn't dimmed — it's just seasoned. The world keeps changing, but you've already proven you can, too. So keep walking, keep talking, keep showing up. Adopt the pet, take the class, pour the single glass of wine, dance a little when nobody's watching. You don't have to chase youth; you just have to stay alive in your own story.

Part XI — Resetting the Season

Start now, not on January 1.

So now what? You don't wait until New Year's. New Year's resolutions are promises for tomorrow. Life changes start now—yes, right now. (Finish the book, of course, then get busy.) Join the gym or the Y. Take three-minute walks that turn into five, then ten, then "look at me out here striding like I mean it." By spring you'll surprise yourself.

Make the season playful on purpose. Buy a silly Santa hat and wear it to the grocery store. When people smile at you, give them a big one back. You've lived a life—don't be shy about it. Pull on the ugly sweater, set a small tree aglow in the corner of your room, tune the radio to the holiday station, or find a movie that makes you feel twelve again—even if you watch it on Netflix because you're fancy like that. You've earned the right to be bold.

About that smile: people have argued for years about how many muscles it takes (more than a frown? fewer? depends on the grin), but here's the only part that matters—smiling and laughing help you feel better. Laughter loosens tension, gets blood moving, and takes the edge off stress; it's one of the cheapest mood lifters we've got, and there's actual medical ink on that. So if someone hands you a moment that's even a little bit funny, take it and run. Or at least chuckle and keep walking. Mayo Clinic+1

Call the friend you haven't spoken to in a while. Don't make it a summit meeting—make it a giggle. Acknowledge the bumps, then trade the kind of stories that end with, "Lord, we were something, weren't we?" That's not fluff;

connection is health. Loneliness sneaks up on good people, and it's rough on the body, not just the heart. A coffee date, a standing phone call, a neighborly wave—tiny stitches that hold a season together. CDC+1

Keep the "be good to yourself" pieces simple. A single glass of something festive beats three you'll regret. A short walk today beats a perfect plan you never start. And if you feel silly in that Santa hat, remember: the point isn't to impress anyone—it's to wake up your own joy. Even little bits of movement and mood can shift the whole day; you don't need marathons to feel better, but you do need momentum. The Washington Post+1

Make this the holiday of all holidays. Be bold like red, amorous like green, and shine like gold and silver. Smile on purpose. Laugh out loud. And when December leans in and asks,

"How do you want to do this year?"—answer honestly: lighter, kinder, funnier… and starting now.

Holiday Magic Check-In

(Because reflection doesn't have to be solemn
— it can sparkle.)

1. What tradition would you reboot if no one judged you?
Maybe it's putting up the tree in October, baking cookies for breakfast, or skipping the formal dinner for a movie marathon in pajamas. Forget the "shoulds" — what would make you happy?

2. Who haven't you laughed with in too long?
You know exactly who it is. The one who can't finish a story without both of you snorting with laughter. Call them. Text them. Send a goofy meme. Life's too short to keep the fun people on hold.

3. What one thing could make your season lighter — not perfect, just lighter?

Maybe it's saying no to hosting this year. Maybe it's adopting a tiny tree and stringing popcorn like the old days. Maybe it's turning your phone off for one night. Whatever it is, let that be your gift to yourself.

Spark Page

(Because you still do.)

So you've reached the end — now what? Don't just close the book and sigh. This isn't a souvenir. It's a gentle nudge with lipstick on.

Start small. Make December a verb.

Invite two friends for "coffee that accidentally became wine."
Join a choir even if your high notes could clear a room.
Buy that ridiculous inflatable reindeer because you want to, not because the HOA approves.

Still have that Santa hat? Wear it to the pharmacy. Nothing brightens a blood-pressure check like a jingle-bell head.

And if the mirror catches you mid-dance, don't stop. That's endorphins in motion. The Mayo Clinic swears laughter and movement boost your immune system, lower stress hormones, and help you sleep better. They didn't say which dance, so you're medically cleared for the Electric Slide.

Need a creative spark? Write your own "Twelve Days of Freedom."

Day 1 — Sleep late.

Day 2 — Breakfast for dinner.

Day 3 — Forgive someone who never said sorry.

Day 4 — Re-watch It's a Wonderful Life and actually root for Clarence this time.

By Day 12, you'll remember this truth: the good life isn't what you plan — it's what you notice.

And if a quiet, ordinary, gentle moment sneaks up on you — let it. That's holiday magic showing up without an RSVP.

Acknowledgments

Every book is a conversation that starts as a whisper and somehow finds its voice. This one began as a simple idea — a nod to every Boomer who still believes life can sparkle at any age — and turned into a joyful, laugh-out-loud reminder that we are still here.

To every friend who listened, nudged, or said, "You should write that down" — thank you. You did more than encourage me; you gave me permission to play.

To the doctors, researchers, and everyday wise souls whose work informed the facts tucked between the laughs — thank you for reminding us that science and spirit can live happily on the same page.

To AD, who shares the coffee, the calm, and the chaos — thank you for being home.

To the readers — the Boomers, the pre-Boomers, the post-Boomers, and all honorary members — thank you for reading with open hearts and open minds. May your holidays be bold like red, hopeful like green, and as enduring as gold.

And to life itself — for the memories, the reinventions, and the perfectly timed second chances — I'm still raising my glass to you.

— A L Manley

About the Author

A L Manley has seen the world through both work, wonder and pleasure, collecting stories and characters along the way. A native Virginian, Manley blends wisdom, wit, and real talk into narratives that remind readers it's never too late to rewrite the script.

Manley's debut novel, Beneath the Glass, is an introduction to a bold, elegant, and unapologetic grown-up style. Holiday Magic Boomer Style continues that spirit, celebrating reinvention, humor, and the courage to start fresh long after the world expects you to slow down.

Manley writes under the Ink-Twenty Studio imprint, building a catalog that pairs heart with hustle — stories that make you laugh, think, and sometimes tear up, all while enjoying good coffee or an English tea & biscuit.

When not writing, Manley can often be found walking a trail in one of the many state's parks, with Savvy Girl, a devoted German Shepherd and loyal companion.

Ink-Twenty Studio

Richmond, Virginia

Notes & References

(Because even holiday magic deserves fact-checking.)

Money & Retirement

Social Security Administration (SSA) — Full retirement age, early-benefit reduction, and delayed-credit rules: ssa.gov/benefits/retirement

Internal Revenue Service (IRS) — Required Minimum Distribution (RMD) age increases under the SECURE Act 2.0 (2023): irs.gov/retirement-plans

U.S. Department of the Treasury — Lifetime-income and annuity guidelines.

Investopedia — Fixed, variable, and indexed annuity comparisons (2024 edition).

U.S. Department of Labor — 401(k) contribution and withdrawal guidance: dol.gov/agencies/ebsa

Housing & Lifestyle

Del Webb Corporation Archives — History of Sun City, AZ (1960) and the first age-restricted communities.

U.S. Census Bureau — Population growth data for The Villages metro area; 2020 Census highlights.

National Association of Home Builders (NAHB) — 55+ Housing Market Data Report (2024).

AARP Research — Downsizing and aging-in-place trends (2023).

Cultural History & Pop Culture

Library of Congress Archives — Elvis Presley's 1956 television debut and the rise of Motown Records.

Smithsonian Institution — Exhibits on Sears, Kmart, and the American mall era.

Rock & Roll Hall of Fame — Milestones for The Beatles, Motown, and MTV (1980s).

Demographics & Sociology

Pew Research Center — Defining Generations 2024: Boomers and Beyond.

National Institute on Aging (NIA) — Studies on longevity and social engagement.

Health & Well-Being

Centers for Disease Control and Prevention (CDC) — Physical-activity guidelines for adults 65+.

CDC — "Physical Activity and Brain Health" (2023 update).

CDC — "Loneliness and Social Isolation in Older Adults" (2023).

NIA — Nutrition, sleep, and cognitive-health research.

Harvard T.H. Chan School of Public Health — Moderate-alcohol-consumption findings.

American Heart Association (AHA) — Smoking cessation and cardiovascular-risk data for adults over 60.

Human–Animal Bond Research Institute (HABRI) — Pet companionship and reduced loneliness in seniors.

Mayo Clinic — Studies on laughter therapy and stress reduction (2024).

Cleveland Clinic — Research on smiling, facial muscles, and mood improvement (2023).

www.ingramcontent.com/pod-product-compliance
Lightning Source LLC
Chambersburg PA
CBHW020643130626
46552CB00003B/1368